In memory of my mum,
who taught me to sew.
C. B.

To all the babies of my
family and friends.
L. G.

First published 2015 by Walker Books Ltd
87 Vauxhall Walk, London SE11 5HJ

2 4 6 8 10 9 7 5 3 1

Text © 2015 Chris Butterworth Illustrations © 2015 Lucia Gaggiotti

This book has been typeset in VAG Rounded

Printed in Malaysia

British Library Cataloguing in Publication Data:
a catalogue record for this book is available from the British Library

ISBN 978-1-4063-3296-4

www.walker.co.uk

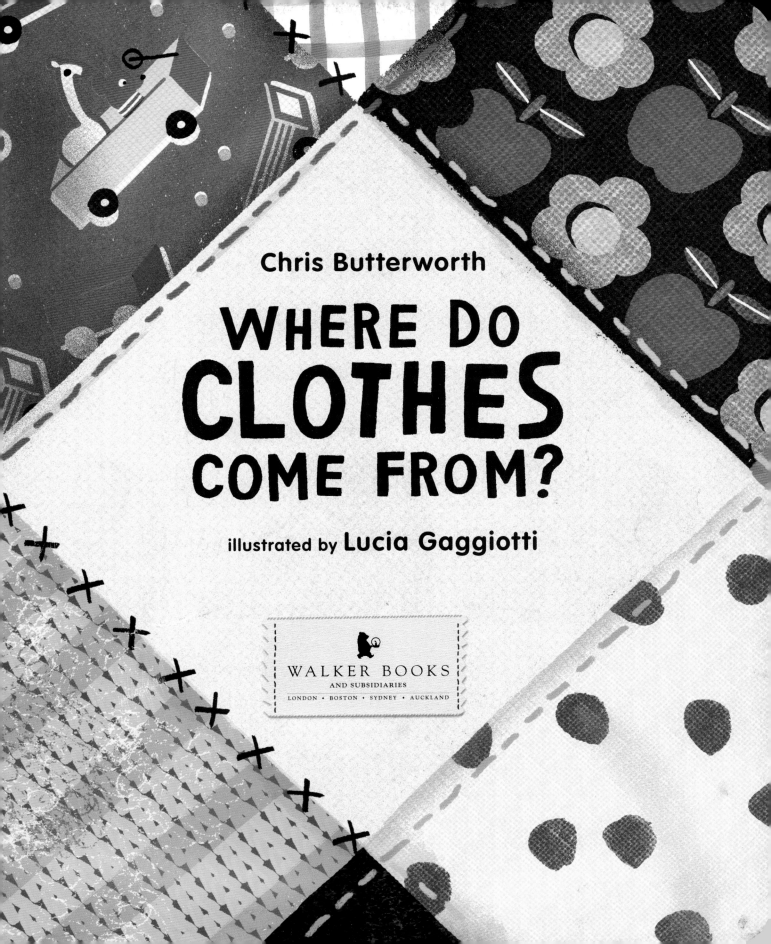

Chris Butterworth

WHERE DO CLOTHES COME FROM?

illustrated by **Lucia Gaggiotti**

WALKER BOOKS
AND SUBSIDIARIES
LONDON · BOSTON · SYDNEY · AUCKLAND

WOULDN'T it be great if you could wear your favourite clothes ALL the time?

But you need different clothes for different weather and for doing different things.

6

You need warm clothes for cold days, cool clothes for hot days, and clothes to keep you dry in the rain.

You need smart clothes and clothes to muck about in.

But what are your clothes made of?

And where do they come from?

WHAT ARE YOUR JEANS MADE OF?

Your jeans are made of cotton, and cotton grows on bushes!

A cotton seed needs lots of sun and water to grow into a bush.

It takes about ten weeks for a flower to bloom. After the flower dies, a seed pod, called a cotton boll, swells and ripens.

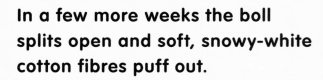

fibres

In a few more weeks the boll splits open and soft, snowy-white cotton fibres puff out.

The bolls are picked (by hand or by machine).

cotton & seeds IN

Then a ginning machine gets rid of the seeds tangled in the cotton fibres.

The cleaned cotton is baled up and taken to a spinning mill.

cotton OUT

seeds OUT

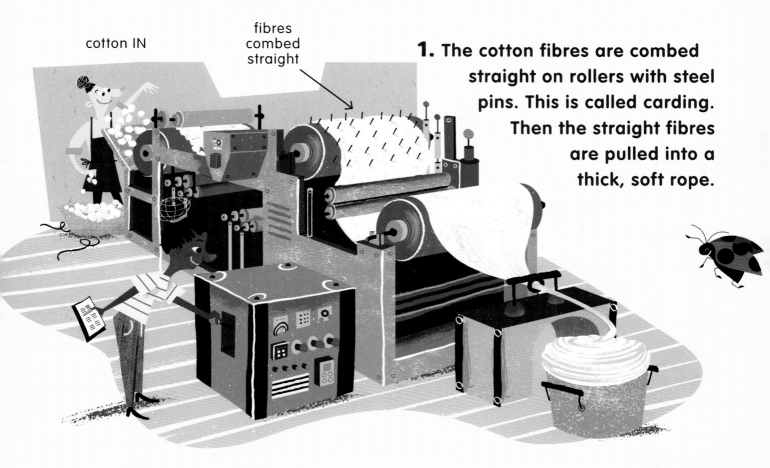

cotton IN

fibres combed straight

1. The cotton fibres are combed straight on rollers with steel pins. This is called carding. Then the straight fibres are pulled into a thick, soft rope.

2. Next the spinning machine stretches the fibres …

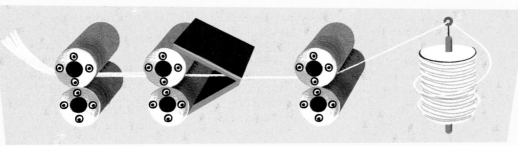

and twists them into a single thread called yarn.

3. In another mill the yarn is dyed in a bath of purply-blue dye.

Now it's ready to be woven into cloth.

The cotton yarn is woven into cloth on a loom.

Then the cloth is cut into shapes ...

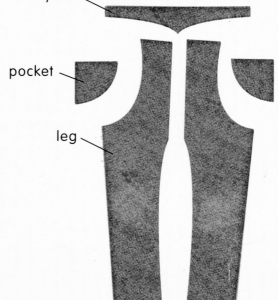

belt loop

waistband

yoke

pocket

leg

which are sewn
together into your **JEANS**.

Your jeans are **COOL**
to wear and **STRONG** enough
to stand up to rough stuff.

Clothes are made from
other plants too.

Linen is
made from
the stalks of flax plants.

It is some of the oldest cloth in the
world. Ancient Egyptians wrapped
their mummies in
it, and the
Romans
wore linen
togas.

The stalks of hemp plants can be
made into cloth, too. It's so strong
that soldiers' uniforms used
to be made of it.

WHAT iS YOUR JUMPER MADE OF?

It's made of wool – the long hair from a sheep. The sheep's wool is cut off once a year (it doesn't hurt the sheep – she's probably glad to be cool again).

Raw wool is dirty and greasy, so it's taken to a mill and washed well.
This is called scouring.

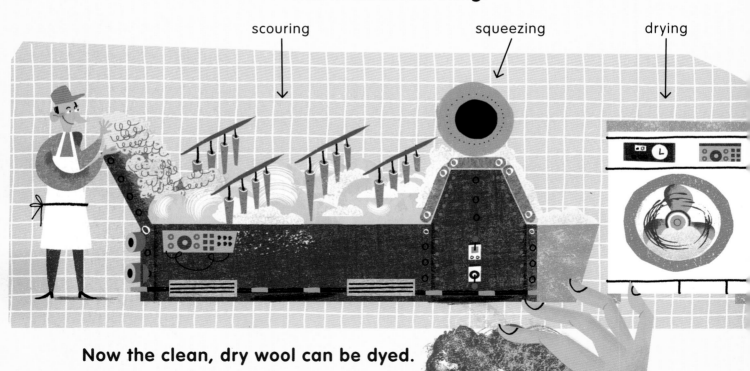

scouring   squeezing   drying

Now the clean, dry wool can be dyed.

The carding machine combs the dry fibres straight and rolls them into a thick, soft rope of wool.

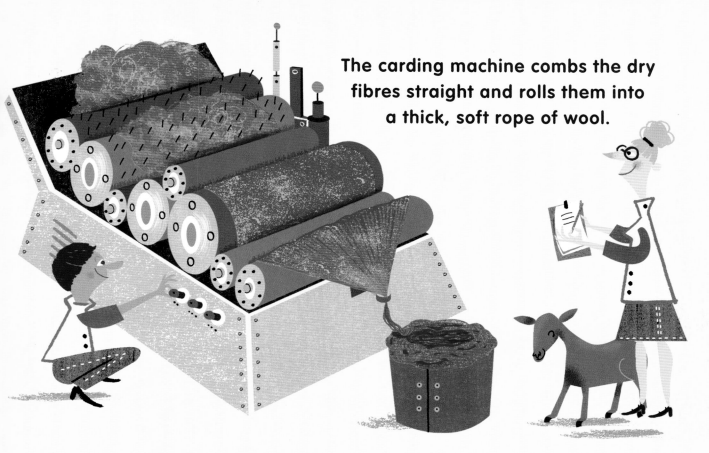

Next the spinning machine gently pulls out the stretchy wool fibres and twists them into yarn.

The yarn is very thin, so several strands are twisted together to make wool that is thick enough to knit into clothes.

You can knit on a machine or by hand. Or maybe someone in your family can knit your jumper!

Here's your **JUMPER**. The wool kept the sheep **WARM**, now it's keeping you cosy!

Around the world people make wool from different long-haired animals.

Yaks in Tibet

Bison in North America

Camels in China

Llamas and alpacas in South America

Musk oxen in Alaska

Cashmere goats grow extra-soft hair that makes silky, fine jumpers.

The hair from curly Angora goats is made into soft mohair wool for clothes – and favourite teddy bears!

Angora rabbit wool is REALLY fluffy!

WHAT iS YOUR **PARTY DRESS** MADE OF?

It's made of silk. Silk is the lightest cloth of all and it's a fibre made by worms!

Silkworms are not really worms – they're the caterpillars of a small white moth.

Farmers breed thousands of them, feeding them on the leaves of mulberry trees.

Each silkworm makes a single silk thread, and winds it into a cocoon round its body. This single thread can be 1.6km long!

The cocoons are dried then softened in hot water.

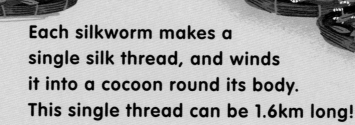

The super-fine silk threads are gently unrolled and wound round a reel.

These silk threads are pulled and twisted together to make a thicker, stronger yarn.

Then the silk is dyed into bright colours and woven into cloth on a loom.

Now it's ready to be made into your **PARTY DRESS**. Silk makes **SPECIAL** cloth: fine, floaty silk; shiny satin and taffeta; rich, furry velvet ... it's perfect for a special occasion.

YOU feel special when you wear it!

WHAT iS YOUR **FOOTBALL KiT** MADE OF?

Your football kit is made of fibres invented by scientists. That's why they're called synthetic or artificial fibres. They have made-up scientific names like polyester, and nylon.

1. Synthetic fibres start as a mixture of chemicals that make a kind of sticky syrup.

2. Inside the machine, this syrup is squeezed through tiny holes into thin strands which harden into fibres.

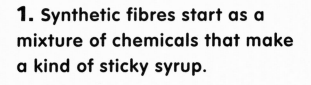

3. The fibres are pulled over rollers and twisted to make a thicker, stronger yarn. Then the yarn is wound onto reels.

Now the yarn is ready to be dyed and woven into cloth.

reel

Cloth made of synthetics is great for **SPORTS CLOTHES**: they **WASH** easily, **DRY** fast, and don't need ironing. (So whoever washes your clothes loves synthetics too!)

3 WHAT IS YOUR **FLEECE** MADE OF?

Don't throw away your plastic bottles: if you recycle them they can be turned into a fleece! It takes about 12 bottles to make your fleece.

At the recycling plant, the plastic is sorted into different colours,

chopped into tiny bits,

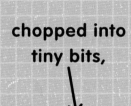

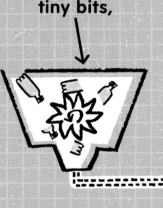

washed ...

and dried.

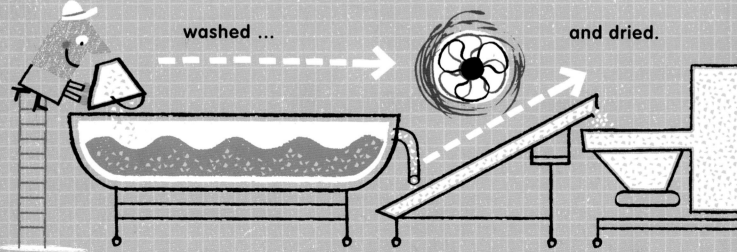

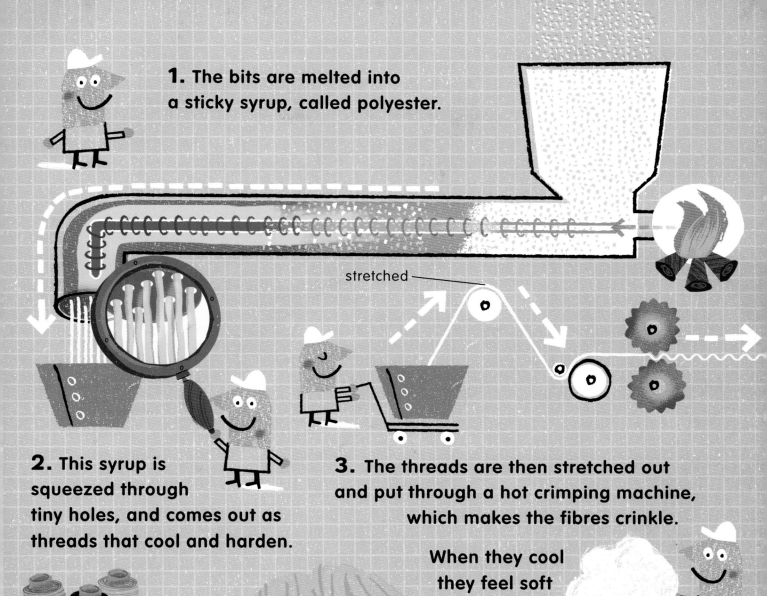

1. The bits are melted into a sticky syrup, called polyester.

stretched

2. This syrup is squeezed through tiny holes, and comes out as threads that cool and harden.

3. The threads are then stretched out and put through a hot crimping machine, which makes the fibres crinkle.

When they cool they feel soft and fluffy, like wool.

4. The fibres are carded, spun and dyed then knitted into cloth. The cloth is then brushed hard on one side to make it fluff up.

Your **FLEECE** keeps out chilly winds: zip it up and stay **SNUG**!

WHAT ARE YOUR WELLiES MADE OF?

Wellies are made from rubber – a juice that comes from a tree!

Rubber trees grow in hot, rainy forests, and inside their bark flows a sticky white juice called latex.

Every day workers make a long cut in the bark of each tree (it's called 'tapping') so the latex runs down and drips into a cup.

The latex is then mixed with acid.

This makes a lumpy mixture which is poured into moulds.

It sets and dries into hard blocks.

1. The blocks of rubber are taken to a factory, and pushed through hot rollers.

2. This is done over and over again until the rubber is in soft, stretchy sheets.

3. As it gets smoother, colours are mixed in.

4. Then the rubber is put through another roller and rolled out into thinner sheets.

5. Boot shapes are cut from the sheets.

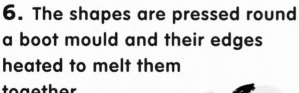

6. The shapes are pressed round a boot mould and their edges heated to melt them together.

Pop on your **WELLIES** and stomp about in the puddles – they are waterproof so your feet stay **DRY**!

RECYCLING FACTS

Have you got clothes you've grown out of or just don't love any more?

In the richer parts of the world we throw away **MILLIONS** of tons of clothes every year.

That's a waste – don't just dump those clothes: **RECYCLE** them! Put them in a recycling bin. (The clothes are chopped up so the fibres can be made into cloth wipes or mattress filling. Synthetic fibres are recycled simply by being melted down again.)

OR

 Your clothes could fit somebody else!

 Use the cloth to make useful things.

 Take them to a charity shop.

 Turn them into something new – cut down old jeans to make shorts or a skirt!

CHARITY SHOP

AUTHOR'S NOTE

I collect cloth from around the world – I love the colours,
the patterns and how different fabrics feel to touch.
It's amazing to think you can take animal hair or part of
a plant, spin it into thread, and then weave, knit or sew it
to make something to wear. Magic!

ILLUSTRATOR'S NOTE

I loved illustrating this book and hope that when children read it
they will realize there's a great story behind everything they wear.

BiBLiOGRAPHY

The Fleece and Fibre Sourcebook (2011)
by Deborah Robson & Carol Ekarius, published
by Storey Publishing

A Cotton T-shirt (How it's Made) (2009)
by Sarah Ridley, published by Franklin Watts

The Biography of Silk (2006)
by Carrie Gleason, published by Crabtree Publishing

iNDEX